Text copyright © 1999 by Carol Diggory Shields
Illustrations copyright © 1999 by Scott Nash

First edition 1999

Library of Congress Cataloging-in-Publication Data

Shields, Carol Diggory.
Martian rock / Carol Diggory Shields ; illustrated by Scott Nash. – 1st ed.
p.   cm.
Summary: A group of Martians looking for life on the different planets in the solar system
make a surprising discovery just as they are about to give up.
ISBN: 0-7636-0598-0
[1. Life on other planets – Fiction. 2. Planets – Fiction. 3. Penguins – Fiction.
4. Stories in rhyme.] I. Nash, Scott, ill.   II. Title.
PZ8.3.S55365Mar 1999
[E] – dc21   98-51123

2 4 6 8 10 9 7 5 3 1

Printed in Hong Kong / China

This book was typeset in Apache.
The illustrations were done in watercolor and pencil.

Candlewick Press
2067 Massachusetts Avenue
Cambridge, Massachusetts 02140

To Tom Corey – S. N.

To Alex – C. D. S.

MARTIAN
ROCK

Carol Diggory Shields

illustrated by

Scott Nash

CANDLEWICK PRESS
CAMBRIDGE, MASSACHUSETTS

"Attention all life forms,
    simple and complex!
Tune in your antennae
    and flex your necks—
Our brave explorers
    of the solar system
Blast off in ten quadsecs,
    and how we will miss them!"

Long had they wondered, on the red planet Mars,
   If life could exist somewhere else in the stars.
Now the moment had come—
   the great engines roared,
And off into space the voyagers soared.

Their first destination
was Orb Number Nine,
The outermost planet,
so the trip took some time.

It was dreary and dark,
   and mostly all granite.
They radioed home—
   "No life on this planet."

They flew on to Eight,
   the one that's deep blue,
And counted eight moons.
   (Mars only has two.)
Winds howled and whistled
   in storms of blue snow.
Not a life form in sight
   at four hundred below.

Many moons circled Seven
  (they counted fifteen),
As it rolled on its side
  and glowed sickly green.
It was slushy and smelly,
  with no living things.
So they went on to Six,
  with the bright yellow rings.

Those rings were just junk,
    and the planet just gas.
There was no place to land,
    so they flew right on past.

Orb Five was red-orange,
    magnetic, immense,
And covered with clouds
    that were swirling and dense.

Amid thunder and lightning,
    they decided to beat it.
"If anything lives here,
    we don't want to meet it!"

They stepped on the gas,
    sped toward the Sun,
And didn't slow down until they got to Orb One.

Orb Number One
    was hotter than blazes
So they set off for Two,
    which was covered with hazes.

Orb Two was much hotter,
with acid rain pelting.

They knew they should leave
when the ship started melting.

By now they were homesick,
filled with despair,
And fresh out of socks
and clean underwear.

"There's nobody out here.
We're all alone.
We'll look at Orb Three,
then head for home."

They buzzed the south pole,
saw nothing but snow.
"It's cold and it's empty," they sighed.
"Let's just go."

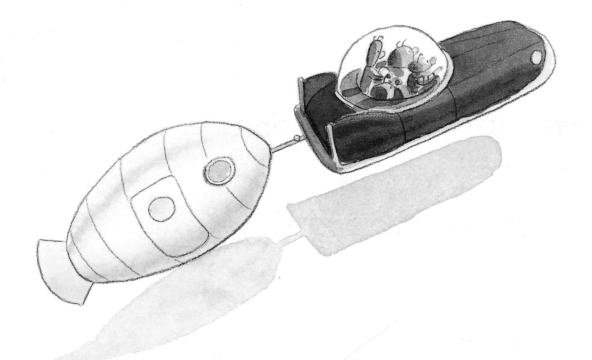

Then as the crew sagged, the captain declared,
"Wait just one quadsec—
there's something out there!"

They looked out the window
and saw he was right—
An alien life form strolled slowly in sight!
It came right to the ship
with a waddling walk
And greeted the crew
with a nod and a squawk.

Then from the horizon more came by the dozens:
Grandparents, babies, aunts, uncles, and cousins.
They surrounded the craft in a jostling pack.
The Martians were scared; were they under attack?

But the life forms were friendly and quite unafraid.
The Martians soon joined in the games that they played,

Like Follow-the-Leader

and Slippery-Sliding,

Tummy-Toboggan and

Find-Me-I'm-Hiding.

They showed off their diving, invited them in.
(The Martians said no because Martians can't swim.)

So the Martians phoned home.

"We need wonder no more—
Life has been found
on the planet
next door!"

Their mission accomplished, the crew had to go.
"We'll miss you," they said to their friends in the snow.
"Just keep on evolving—some day you might fly!
Then come visit *us*—our orb is close by."

Then they left their new friends
with a fine souvenir:
A lasting reminder that
The Martians were here!

Martian name: **MARTIAN ROCK**
(a fine souvenir)
Earth name: **ALH 84001**

ALH 84001, a six-inch-long meteorite believed to be from Mars, was found on Antarctica in 1984. Antarctica is one of the best places on Earth to find meteorites because, among other reasons, they're easy to spot on Antarctica's many ice fields. Thousands of meteorites have been discovered there, some of which are thought to be from Mars. But ALH 84001 is unlike any other Martian meteorite. Scientists discovered microscopic features in it that resemble ancient bacteria on Earth. This discovery sparked a debate about whether or not these may be fossils of ancient Martian life — a debate that is still going on today!

Pluto is the farthest planet from the Sun—most of the time. But its orbit does, at times, bring Pluto closer to the Sun than the next nearest planet, Neptune. Pluto has a bluish color and one very large moon, Charon. Its surface is quite dark in places, but brighter in areas covered by solid ices of nitrogen, methane, and carbon monoxide. The temperature is, on average, a very chilly -382°F!

Martian name: **ORB 9 PLUTO**
Earth name:

Martian name: **ORB 8**
Earth name: **NEPTUNE**

Neptune has the strongest winds of any of the planets. Giant hurricanes circle the planet, and one of them is as wide as the Earth! And because Neptune is so far from the Sun, the average temperature is about -364°F. The planet has eight moons, and gets its deep blue color from methane gas in its very cloudy atmosphere.

Martian name: **ORB 7**
Earth name: **URANUS**

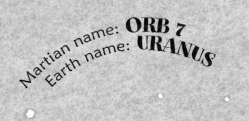

Uranus is the only planet that doesn't rotate on its north and south poles, but tilted on its side. The planet has at least ten rings and fifteen moons. Uranus is believed to have a small, rocky core surrounded by an unpleasant combination of water, ammonia, and methane gases and ices.

Martian name: **ORB 6**
Earth name: **SATURN**

While no one knows for sure what Saturn's rings are made of, some believe it's probably a combination of ice chunks, snowballs, and possibly pieces of shattered moons. Saturn is mostly made up of hydrogen, with smaller amounts of helium and methane. It has eighteen known moons—and the Hubble Space Telescope recently spotted four new objects orbiting the planet that might be moons as well!

Jupiter is the largest planet in the solar system. The planet has a strong magnetic field that stretches out millions of miles into space, and a powerful, ever-changing system of clouds and storms. One of these storms, the Great Red Spot, may be up to 300 years old, and in places is twice as wide as the Earth. Jupiter has sixteen moons, and scientists believe one of them, Europa, might have a water ocean lurking beneath its icy surface—the possibility of life existing here is under investigation!

Martian name: **ORB 5** Earth name: **JUPITER**

Toward the end of the 18th century, scientists predicted that there should be another planet between the orbits of Jupiter and Mars. In time, it was discovered that there are actually many smaller objects, asteroids, orbiting the Sun in this region. Some of these asteroids might have been captured by the pull of Mars and Jupiter, becoming moons of the two planets.

Martian name: **THE ASTEROID BELT**
Earth name: **THE ASTEROID BELT**

Martian name: **ORB 3**
Earth name: **EARTH**

Like Mars, Earth has a very varied landscape. Unlike Mars, Earth's atmosphere is made up mostly of nitrogen, with smaller amounts of oxygen, and it has water oceans. Earth is teeming with life forms "simple and complex"—from redwood trees to raccoons, penguins to plankton, and hippopotamuses to humans.

Martian name: **MARS**
Earth name: **MARS**

Mars is a planet of low-lying plains, giant volcanic mountains, massive canyons, sweeping dunes of red sand, and craters of all sizes. The average temperature is about -81°F, and huge wind storms often rage over large areas of the planet. Mars has two very small moons, Delmos and Phobos, that orbit very close to the planet.

Martian name: **ORB 2**
Earth name: **VENUS**

Venus is covered with thick, swirling clouds; so from a distance, it looks as if it could even be Earth's sister planet. Up close, however, the two planets are very different. Venus is surrounded by a very dense atmosphere of carbon dioxide that traps sunlight and creates a terrible greenhouse effect. As a result, the average surface temperature is a scorching 900°F—even hotter than the temperature on Mercury!

Martian name: **ORB 1**
Earth name: **MERCURY**

Mercury is the closest planet to the Sun. It has almost no atmosphere, so its sky is always black. Mercury is quite warm—on average around 345°F. Its surface looks a lot like that of Earth's moon, with dusty hills and ancient craters of all sizes marking the surface.

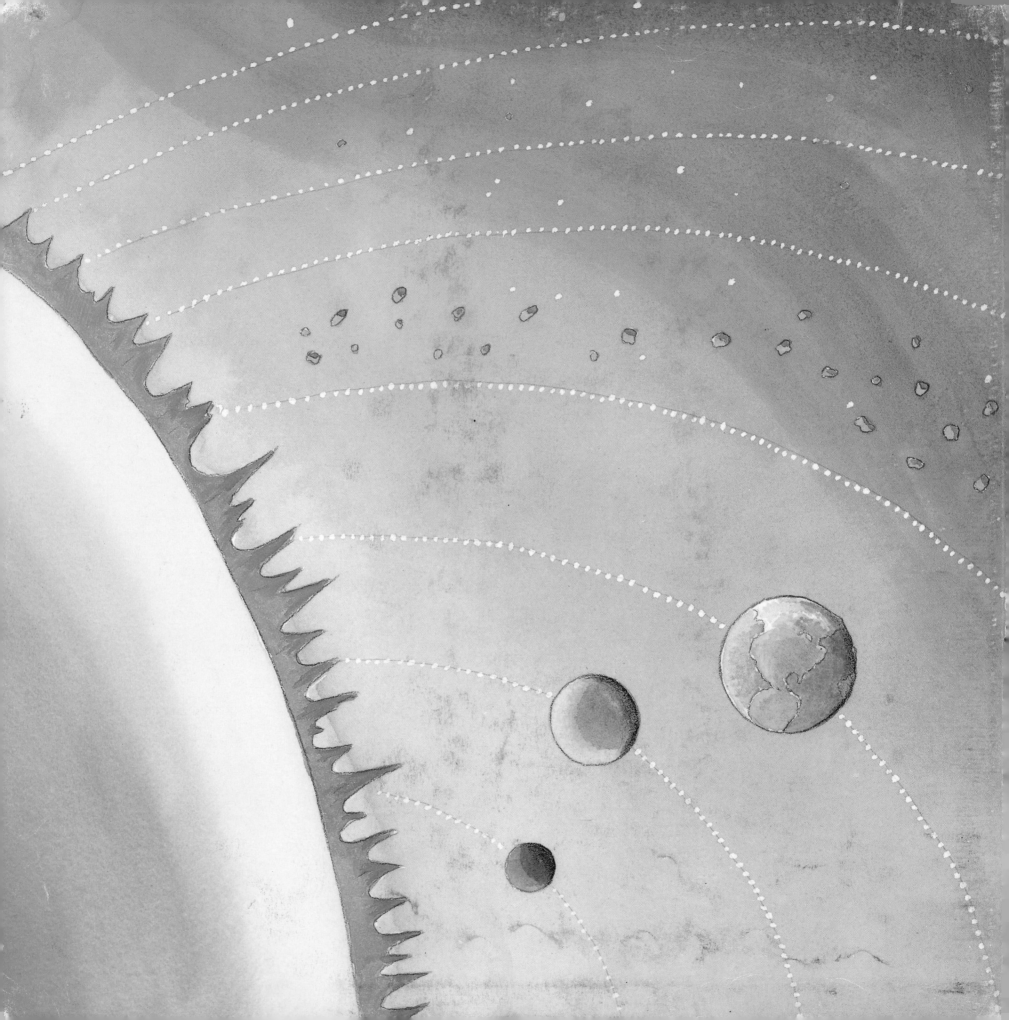